OUR AMAZING UNIVERSE

Written by Arwen Hubbard and Jennifer Swanson
Models designed and built by Simon Pickard, Tim Goddard, Nate Dias, and Jason Briscoe

This LEGO® book belongs to

....

I celebrated World Book Day® 2025 with this gift from my local bookseller and DK.

WORLD BOOK DAY®

World Book Day's mission is to offer every child and young person the opportunity to read and love books by giving you the chance to have a book of your own.

To find out more, and for fun activities including video stories, audiobooks and book recommendations, visit worldbookday.com

World Book Day® is a charity sponsored by National Book Tokens.

Contents

WHY DON'T ASTRONAUTS GET HUNGRY?
BECAUSE THEY'VE HAD A BIG LAUNCH!

Introduction

Welcome to the universe! We have only just begun to explore it. So far, we know it is a very, very big place, full of swirling galaxies, shining stars, mysterious black holes, and, of course, the little blue planet we call home. Earth is an incredibly diverse place and is the only planet in our Solar System that is capable of sustaining life, which makes it extremely special. Let's take a look around and see what there is to discover.

HOW DO YOU ORGANIZE A SPACE PARTY?
YOU PLAN-ET!

Where did everything come from?

Scientists think that 13.8 billion years ago, everything in our universe was squeezed together in a hot, dense state. Suddenly the universe started to expand in a moment known as the Big Bang. As the universe grew and cooled, atoms formed and became the building blocks of stars, planets, galaxies, and us.

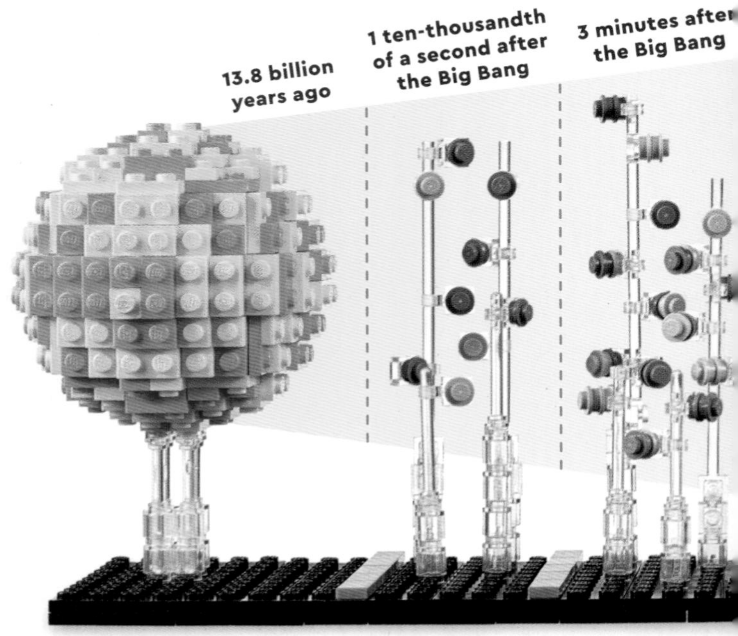

Getting bigger

The universe has continued to expand since the Big Bang. Scientists are working hard to learn more about the early universe and how it has changed over time. Recent observations of faraway galaxies show that the expansion of the universe is speeding up as it gets older and bigger.

COVER YOUR EARS – IT'S THE BIG BANG!

WOW!
Space is expanding **everywhere** at once. There is no centre of the universe.

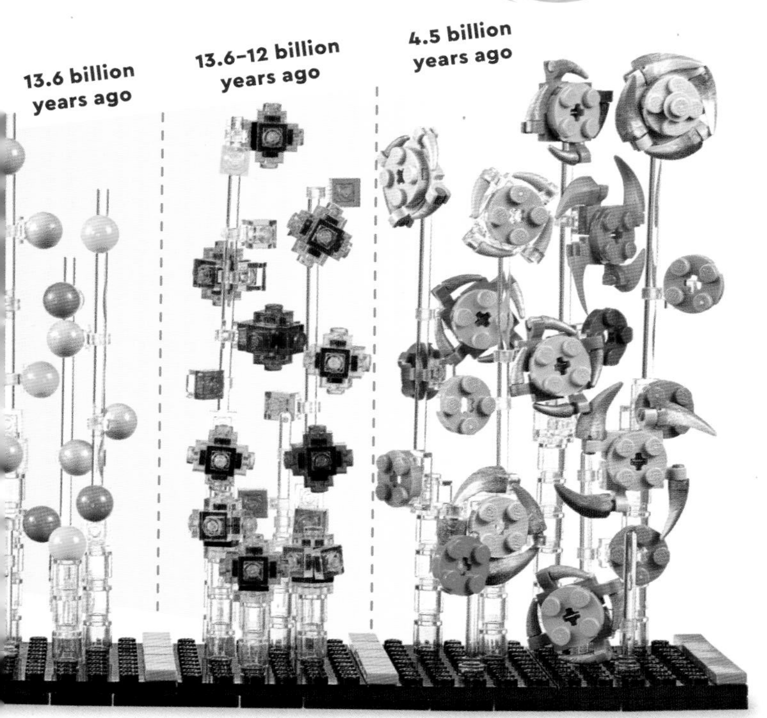

The first stars start to shine

Galaxies begin to form

Modern galaxies – the Solar System is born

What is space made of?

Space is full of amazing objects like stars, black holes, nebulae, planets, and asteroids. Even though there are lots of things in space, it is mostly empty because things are really far apart from each other. Everything in space is made from matter and energy. We think all the energy in the universe has existed since the Big Bang. Energy can't be created or destroyed – it just changes from one form to another.

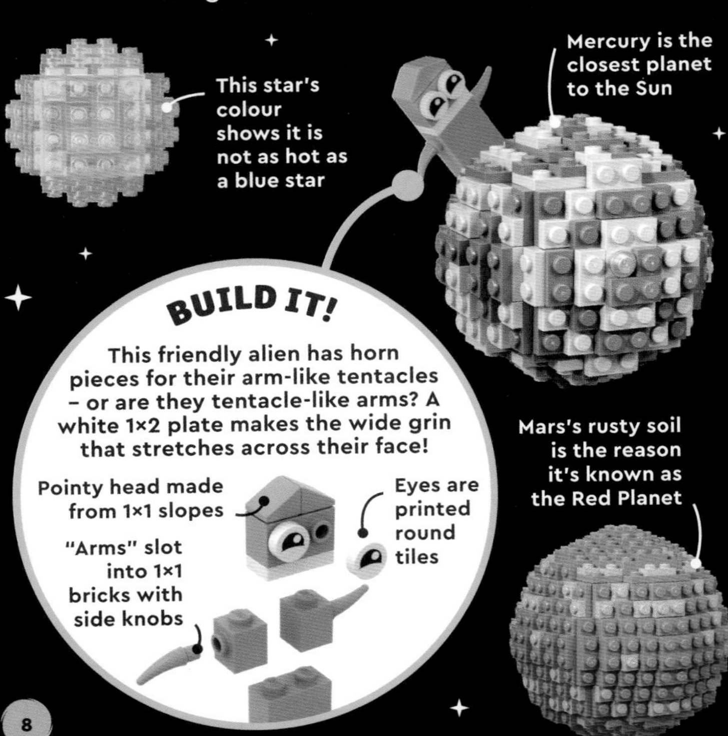

Do you think there is other life out there? What would it look like? Build the **funniest-looking alien** you can imagine.

Earth is the only planet in our Solar System where liquid water is found on the surface

A comet has a blue gas tail and a white dust tail

Black holes occur when stars collapse

WOW! I DON'T KNOW WHERE TO LOOK FIRST!

Matter and energy

Matter is the stuff that things are made from. Stars, planets, and people are made from a kind of matter called elements. Elements are like LEGO® bricks; you can put them together in different ways to create new things! Energy is something stuff has when it is moving, or could be moving, like when a spring is pushed down ready to pop up.

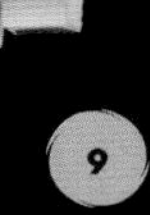

How big is space?

We know that space is really, REALLY big. But scientists don't agree on how big the universe is yet. Some think that it is infinitely big – meaning it goes on forever! Others think that it must have a finite (or limited) size. What scientists do agree on is that there are hundreds of billions of galaxies, each with billions of stars in them.

REALLY!

Whenever you look at the night sky, you are looking **back in time**! It takes time for the stars' light to travel across space to your eyes.

BUILD IT!

This ship's impressive engine housing is made from two LEGO® Technic pieces threaded onto a LEGO Technic axle. One end of the axle plugs into a cross-hole brick at the back of the main hull.

LEGO Technic axle

LEGO Technic wheel

LEGO Technic turbine wheel

It takes a spacecraft just a few minutes to get into orbit

Did you know?

One way to think about the size of space is in terms of LEGO minifigures! You would need to stack 9.5 billion astronaut minifigures to reach from Earth to the Moon, and 9.5 trillion to get all the way to Mars!

Where are we in space?

We live on a small planet called Earth, orbiting (going around) a small star called the Sun, which is orbiting the centre of a galaxy called the Milky Way. All the things that orbit around the Sun are part of the Solar System. As the Sun travels through the Milky Way, it brings everything in the Solar System along with it.

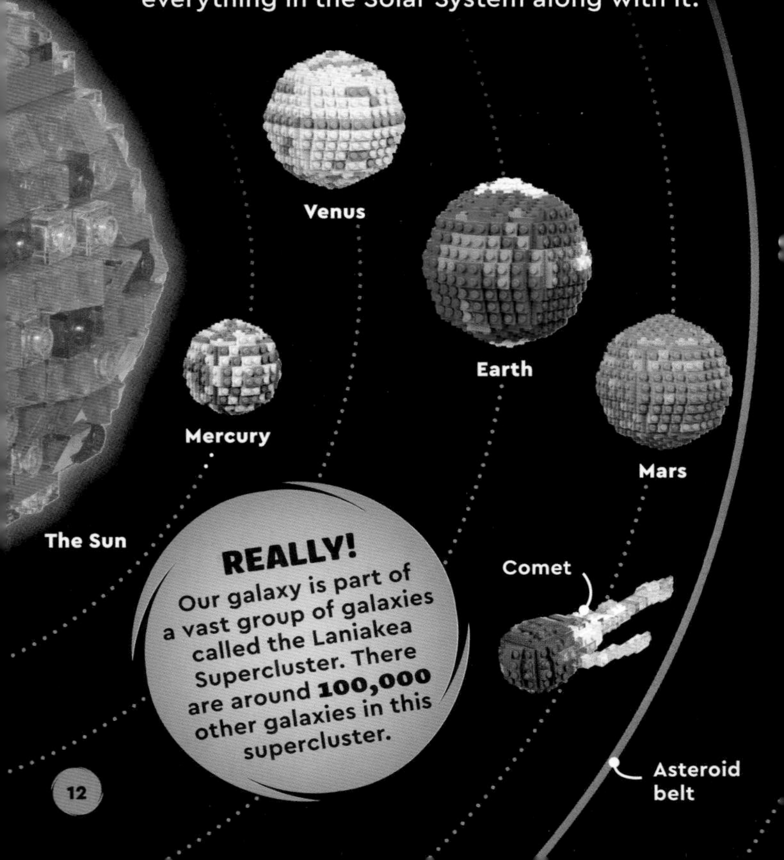

REALLY!
Our galaxy is part of a vast group of galaxies called the Laniakea Supercluster. There are around **100,000** other galaxies in this supercluster.

Earth's position

The Solar System has different zones. Earth is in the inner Solar System, which includes everything up to and including the asteroid belt. That means we are close to the Sun, where it is hot. Earth's nearest neighbours are our Moon, Mercury, Venus, and Mars.

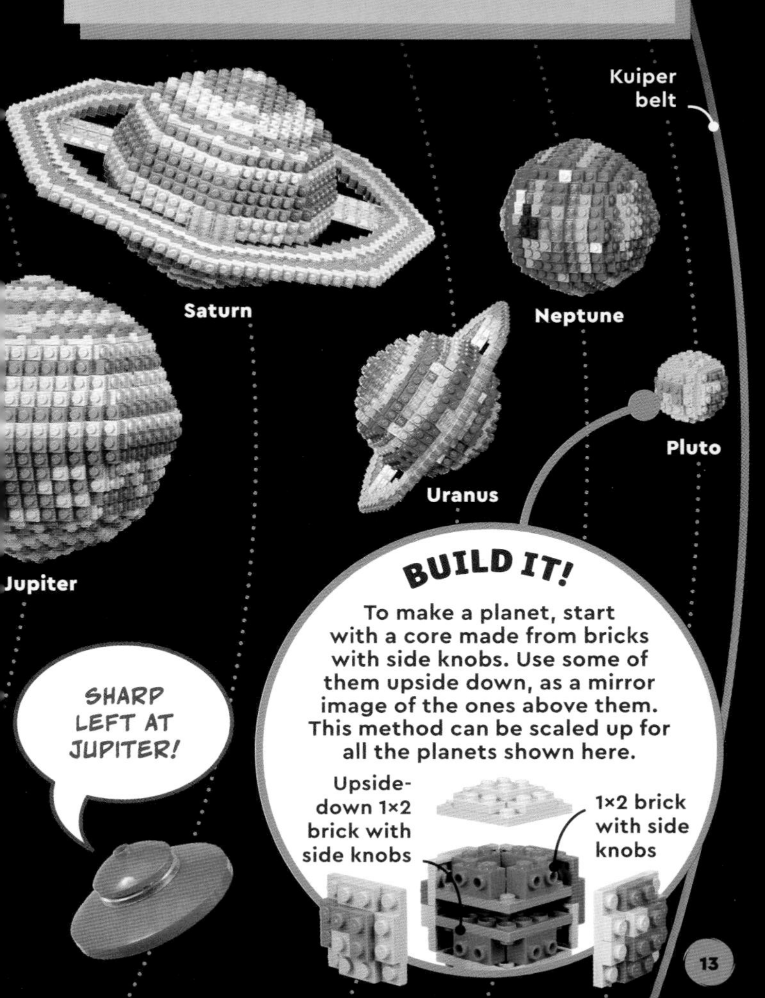

Why is there life on Earth?

Earth has lots of things we don't find in space, such as liquid water to drink and air to breathe. Living beings like humans, other animals, and plants need food and habitats to survive. Earth's ecosystems provide those things. But Earth has not always been a good place for life. Earth has changed a lot over the past 4.5 billion years since it formed. It took millions of years for the ecosystems to grow.

WOW!

Earth probably formed from lots of smaller pieces of **rock** and **metal** that were pulled together by gravity.

IMAGINE!

Can you dream up a beautiful **living thing**, yet to be discovered? Invent an amazing new animal or plant!

BUILD IT!

Put together this penguin's head by building out from a 1×1 brick with side knobs all the way around. A sideways curved slope makes the smooth back of the head.

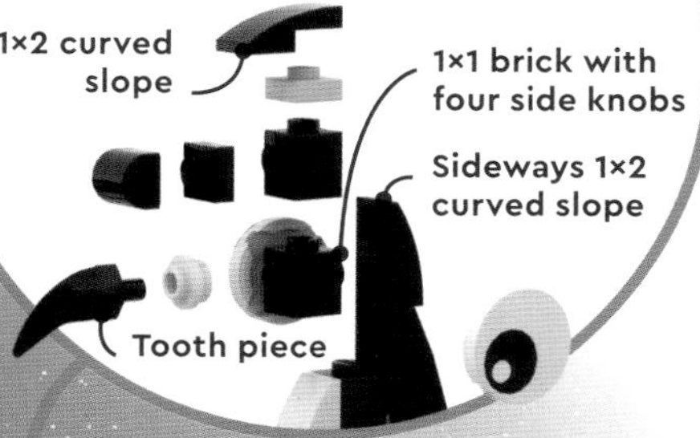

1×2 curved slope

1×1 brick with four side knobs

Sideways 1×2 curved slope

Tooth piece

What is the only star in our Solar System?

It's big, it's yellow (or looks that way to us), and it provides us with the heat we need to survive. It's the Sun! Like all stars, the Sun is a giant ball of hot, glowing gases. It is the closest star to Earth and it is the biggest, brightest object in our sky. While the Sun is the only star in our Solar System, that isn't true for every solar system. Some have two or more! Could you imagine two suns in the sky?

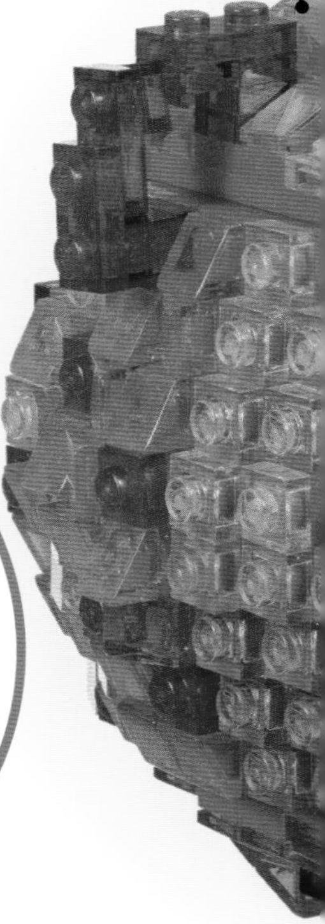

The Sun's surface gives out huge amounts of light, heat, and other energy

BUILD IT!

Is it raining outside? Build a sunny scene to cheer up your day. Using transparent elements makes the Sun appear to float in the sky!

Small bricks create a miniature landscape

Transparent bar

2×2 round brick with axle hole

Sizzling ball

The Sun is thought to be made up of many layers. The centre of the Sun is like a giant bomb that is constantly exploding, creating energy. The Sun has a mind-boggling temperature of 15 million°C (27 million°F) at its core.

Jets of gas shoot out from the surface

Energy from the Sun's core moves very slowly through the Sun's inner layers – it can take 10,000 years to reach the Sun's surface!

WOW!
The Sun is so big that **1.3 million** Earths could fit inside it.

The Sun's energy is created by a nuclear reaction in its core

Why is the Moon so important?

Without that big, bright, grey object in the night sky, life on Earth would be very different. In fact, there may not have been any life at all. Our Moon's gravity stops extreme weather and meteor strikes. It ensures that seasons don't change suddenly and it also slows Earth's rotation so that our days are 24 hours long. The Moon causes Earth's oceans to rise and fall, which creates tides that move water. Tidal power is a powerful source of renewable energy (energy that comes from a natural source that won't run out).

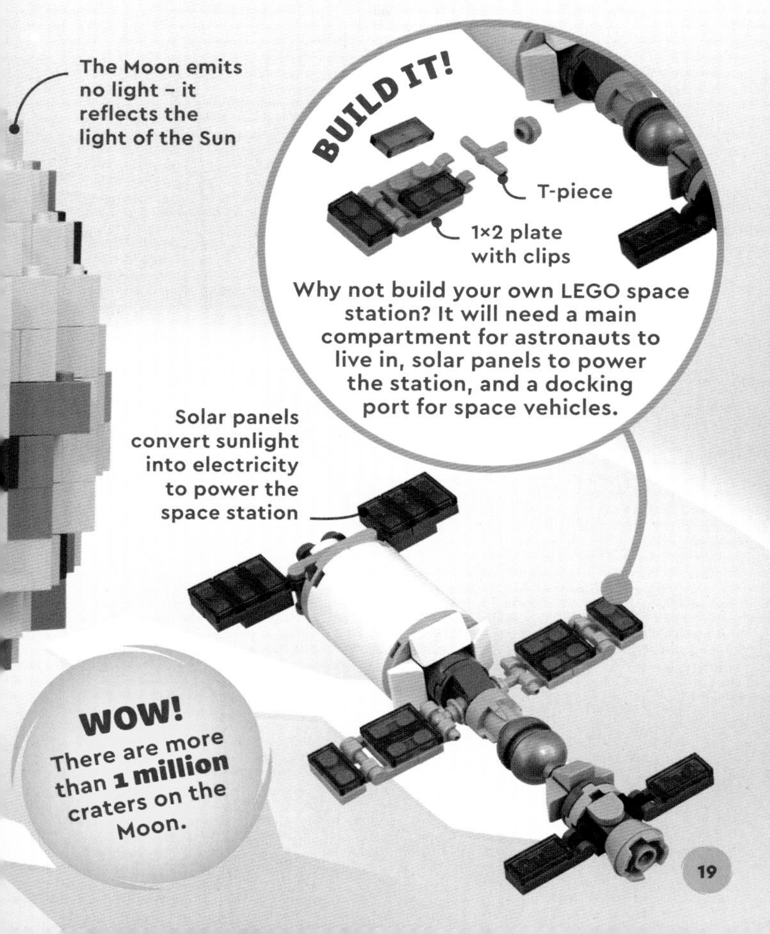

What lies beneath our feet?

Below our feet, Earth is made up of layers – like an apple! The layers are the crust, the mantle, the outer core, and the inner core. The outermost layer is the crust, which is made up of rock. Under the crust is the mantle, where liquid rock, or magma, constantly swirls. These movements shift the crust, causing earthquakes and volcanoes. Inside the mantle is Earth's core. This is made up of an outer core of extremely hot, liquid metal and a solid inner core.

At the centre of it all

Earth's inner core is a mostly solid ball of metal that is intensely hot – with temperatures as high as 6,000°C (10,800°F). That's as hot as the surface of the Sun!

Why do continents move?

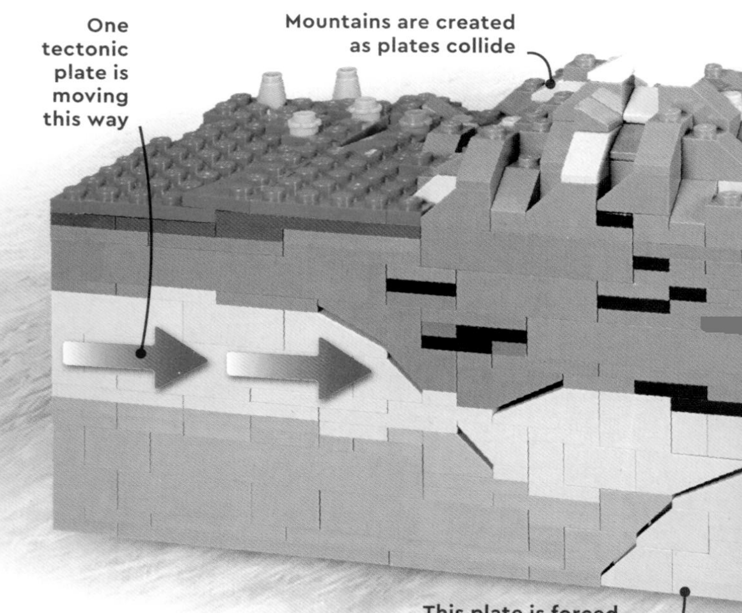

Rubbing together

Two plates may slide past each other horizontally and rub together. The energy created by this can cause earthquakes!

Continents rest on huge, flat pieces of rock called tectonic plates. These plates float on extremely hot, liquid rock contained below the Earth's surface in the mantle. As the superheated liquid moves up and down, it causes the plates to move. The plates move too slowly for us to notice. But you may feel the powerful movements that are triggered when the plate edges meet. This can cause earthquakes and volcanoes, and it transforms the surface of our planet.

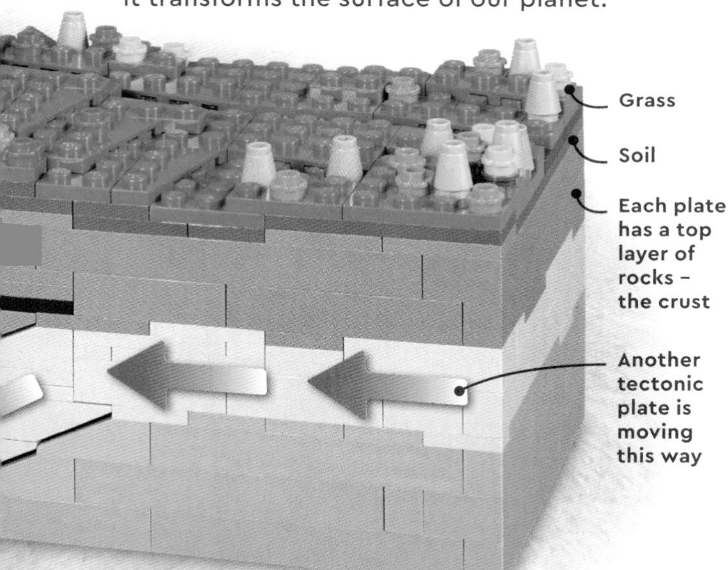

Pushing together

Two plates may meet head-on and push against each other (see above). One plate is pushed under the other, forming a mountain – or even a volcano! This is how Mount Everest, the world's tallest mountain, was created.

REALLY!
The plates that pushed together to form Mount Everest are still moving. This is why the mountain grows **6.4 cm** (2.5 in) every year!

How do volcanoes erupt?

In the mantle, just below Earth's crust, hot, liquid rock, called magma, churns. It dives deep and then rises to the top, looking for a way out. The weight of the crust keeps the lid on the magma, until... a plate in the crust shifts. Whoosh! Magma pushes through the gap and escapes into the volcano above. Pressure from below shoots the magma, now called lava, into the air. Not all eruptions are like this. Some can be (relatively!) calm. If the magma is thin and runny, lava gently oozes out of the top.

WOW!
More than **80 per cent** of the Earth's surface, above and below sea level, came from volcanoes.

A volcano's main vent is often at the top of a mountain
Lava glows bright red when it first erupts
BUILD IT!
Slopes and bricks form a rough, rocky mountain shape. Add orange and red slopes for a stream of lava. You could use transparent red or orange bricks to look extra fiery, or add white bricks on top for clouds of ash.
1×2 plate with bars
1×2 plate with clip
The magma chamber is full of superhot liquid rock

Why do earthquakes happen?

Earth's crust is not one continuous piece of land. It is broken up into giant parts called tectonic plates. These plates shift due to the semi-liquid mantle that constantly moves beneath them. Sometimes the plates push against each other, slide under each other, or move back and forth against each other. All of this motion below causes rumbles and shakes on Earth's surface. Most earthquakes are felt as minor ground-shaking tremors, if at all. But a small number can be earth-shattering.

WOW!
There are around **2,500** earthquakes on Earth every day. Most are too weak to be felt.

Buildings may collapse when there is a strong earthquake

Ring of Fire

The horseshoe-shaped area in the Pacific Ocean, known as the "Ring of Fire", is the site of around 90 per cent of all of the world's earthquakes. Why? It's where the Pacific Plate in Earth's crust meets three other tectonic plates that push and slide against each other.

An earthquake can cause large cracks to open in Earth's surface

How much of Earth is covered by oceans?

Almost three-quarters of Earth is covered by water, and most of that – over 96 per cent – is found in the oceans and seas. Oceans and seas are both large areas of salt water, but oceans are usually much bigger than seas. Oceans span huge distances and reach depths greater than the tallest mountains. Many parts of the oceans are still to be explored.

The oceans are the five largest areas of seawater on Earth and are all connected to each other

Why is the ocean blue?

Sunlight looks white, but it contains many different colours – like a rainbow. When sunlight shines on the sea, different colours get absorbed at different depths. The ocean appears blue because the water absorbs the red part of sunlight first. When the red part is absorbed, our eyes see blue or sometimes blueish-green.

REALLY!
We know more about space than the ocean. We've explored less than **5 per cent** of the oceans on Earth.

Smaller areas of seawater are called seas – they are shallower and smaller than oceans and are usually surrounded by land

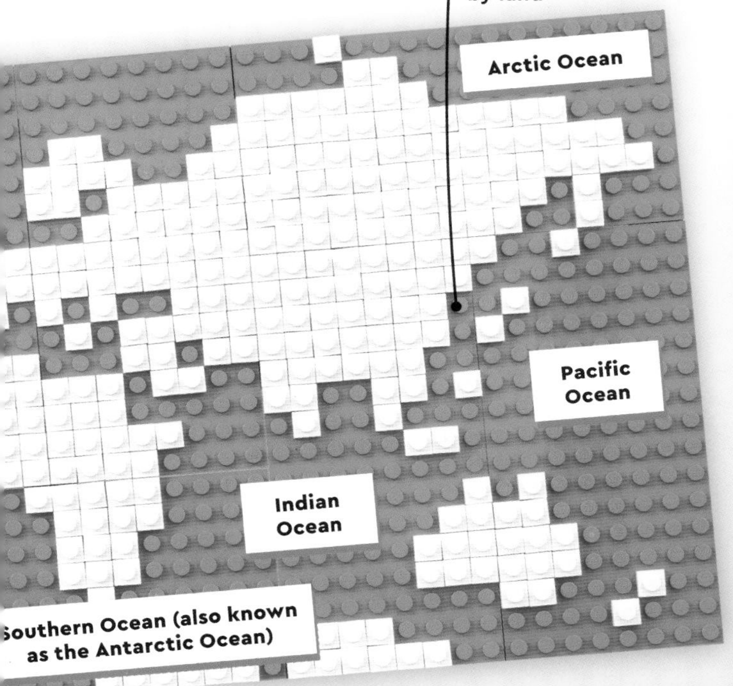

What lurks below?

Deep beneath the ocean's surface is a wild and wonderful world filled with unique creatures who live in extreme cold. Light from the Sun doesn't reach depths below 1,000 m (3,280 ft), so it's also completely dark down there. That doesn't bother these creatures, though, as many of them are bioluminescent, meaning they use chemicals in their bodies to make light. Animals who live in this region are difficult to spot as they can dive to great depths – far deeper than most humans can go!

The fangtooth has the biggest teeth compared to its size of any fish

Hatchet fish have bulging eyes to help spot prey in the dark

REALLY!

The sperm whale's huge head houses the **heaviest brain** of any animal.

Sperm whales have small, beady eyes

Giant squid have eight arms and two long tentacles

IMAGINE!

What's the most incredible **deep-sea animal** you can dream up? Grab your bricks and build it!

Are coral reefs alive?

BUILD IT!

Recreate coral reefs with your most colourful and interesting pieces. Plant, flower, and tentacle pieces work well for coral, but stacking colourful round plates in interesting ways looks effective, too.

2×2 round plates

Coral reefs might look like colourful masses of rock and plants, but coral is actually a living animal. It is made up of thousands of tiny sea creatures called polyps. They eat small animals called zooplankton that they capture in their tentacles. As the polyps grow, they create a hard limestone skeleton. When they die, these skeletons form the hard basis of the coral reef, and new polyps grow on it. Plants called algae also live inside polyps. Algae use the Sun to make sugar for energy, which the polyps eat as food. The polyps then give the algae the carbon dioxide that they need. It's a perfect partnership!

Corals produce colourful pigments when in bright sunlight
Colourful algae inside polyps also give coral its colour
WOW!
Only about 1 per cent of the oceans contain coral reefs, but one-quarter of all ocean life depends on them for food and shelter.

What is the world's highest waterfall?

The highest waterfall in the world is Angel Falls in Venezuela, South America. At more than 979 m (3,200 ft) high, it's hard to miss – it's more than twice as tall as New York's Empire State Building! The water from the Río Kerepakupai Merú cascades from an ancient mountain plateau down a sheer drop to the bottom and the river below. The only way to get up to the waterfall is by taking a helicopter or plane. At that height, it would be a tough climb!

Rushing rapids

Waterfalls can form from very fast moving water, called rapids, which flows over rocks. The softer rocks are eroded, or broken down, more quickly, leaving a ledge of hard rocks. Waterfalls form over these higher, harder rocks.

The force of the water erodes the rock

Water falls down the side of the tepui (also known as a tabletop mountain)
THIS IS HANDY! I NEEDED A SHOWER!
REALLY!
Angel Falls is 15 times higher than Niagara Falls on the US-Canadian border.

How does a glacier move?

Glaciers are huge mountains of ice made from frozen snow. And yet, these mountains can move... very slowly. As the weight of the ice pushes down on the bottom of the glacier, sometimes a tiny bit of it begins to melt. The softer ice can move slightly across the ground. As the glacier moves, the friction between the ice and the ground causes more ice to melt just a little. The result is that the glacier moves, typically around 30 cm (1 ft) per day.

Penguin pals

Penguins are well adapted to cold Antarctica, the southernmost continent on Earth. They have layers of blubber that keep them warm, and interlocking feathers that are warm and waterproof. They even stop their feet getting cold by balancing on their heels and tails instead!

REALLY!
Polar bears and penguins never mix. That's because polar bears live in the **Arctic** and penguins live in **Antarctica**.

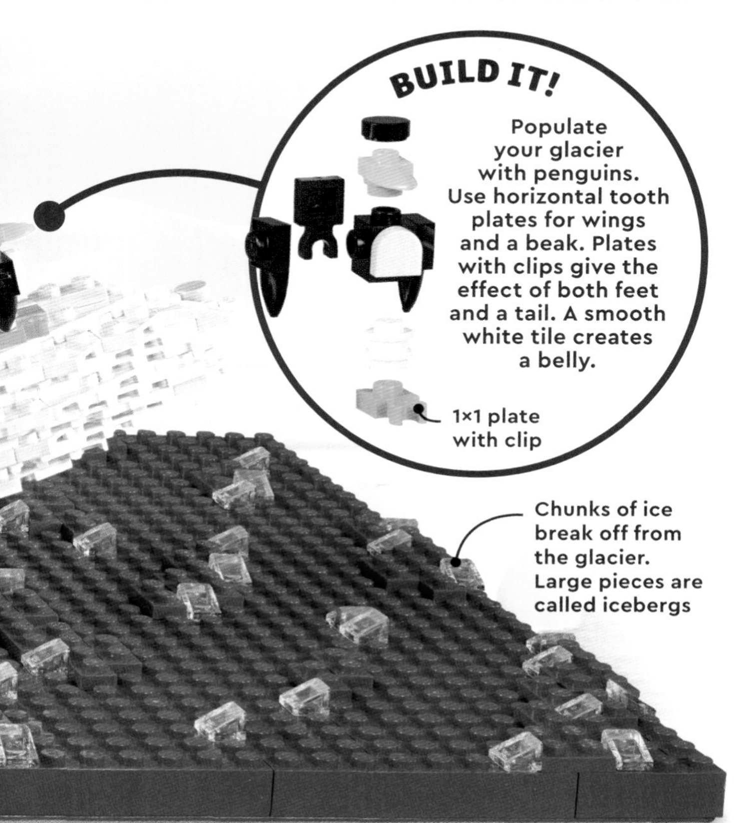

Are deserts always hot?

Most people think of deserts as extremely hot, dry places with sand, but a desert is any region that gets less than 25 cm (10 in) of rain a year. The Sahara in Africa, with its high temperatures, sand dunes, and lack of rain, certainly fits that description. But so does the Gobi Desert in Asia, which is considerably colder, and Antarctica, too. Antarctica gets very little rain and has hardly any plants or wildlife, making it the largest cold desert on our planet.

Bactrian camels live in the Gobi Desert

IMAGINE!

Can you create a new desert-dwelling animal or plant? What would it look like?

Hundreds of dinosaur fossils have been found in the Gobi Desert

Adaptable animals

Animals in the desert, such as the Addax antelope, jerboa, and fennec fox, hunt for food at dawn and dusk to avoid the hottest part of the day. Camels, desert tortoises, and gila monsters can also store water in their bodies so they don't get thirsty.

Fennec fox

The Gobi Desert has relatively little sand – it is mostly stony and rocky

Why do rainforests get so much rain?

Most rainforests are found near the equator, the imaginary line around the centre of the Earth. This is where the Sun's rays hit Earth straight on (rather than at an angle), making it very hot. Heat helps the plants grow, so there are a lot of trees in a rainforest, which leads to a lot of rain. The trees take in water through their roots. The water travels up the tree and is released through the leaves into the atmosphere, forming clouds. Water makes clouds heavy, so the clouds release the water in the form of rain. It's a cycle that happens over and over.

Animal playground

It is thought that around 10 million different species of animals live in rainforests, from tiny green tree ants to large, furry orangutans. There's the poison dart frog, which contains enough poison to kill 10 people, and the red howler monkey, whose voice can be heard 2 km (1.2 miles) away.

Poison dart frog

Red howler monkey

Colourful scarlet macaws fly from tree to tree to feed on fruit and nuts
A giant anteater can catch 35,000 ants in just one day
Armadillos can roll into a ball to hide from predators
WOW!
It can take up to **10 minutes** for a raindrop to reach the ground in a rainforest. Why? So many trees!

Why do we have four seasons?

In many parts of the world, the year has four seasons. This is because Earth is tilted to one side as it orbits (circles around) the Sun. This tilt causes different parts of Earth to lean towards the Sun at different times. When the northern part of our planet is tilted towards the Sun, it is summer there. When the southern part is tilted away from the Sun, it is winter there. As the year goes by, the amount of sunlight that reaches different parts of Earth changes. This gives many places autumn and spring as well as winter and summer.

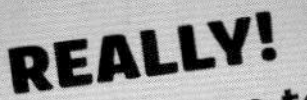

REALLY!

If Earth were to spin upright rather than tilted, we would not have **any seasons.**

In winter, the tree goes into a type of hibernation called dormancy to protect itself and get ready for spring

THIS IS SNOW MUCH FUN!

WOAH! IT'S WINDY TODAY!

Leaves change from green to orange and yellow in the autumn

BUILD IT!

Build a seasonal tree with coloured leaf and flower elements. Think pink and purple florals for spring, green leaves for summer, and orange and red leaves for autumn. For winter, white (snow-covered) flowers will look great next to white tooth-plate icicles.

1×1 vertical tooth plate

1×1 round plate with petals

1×1 round plate with three leaves

What will the cities of the future be like?

Cities of the future could look very different to the ones we know today. They might have buildings with areas of grass or gardens on the roofs. They could be powered with solar power from the Sun. They might be made of renewable materials that help keep the environment clean. Or they might be on space stations like the International Space Station (ISS) – and maybe, one day, there might be a city on the Moon.

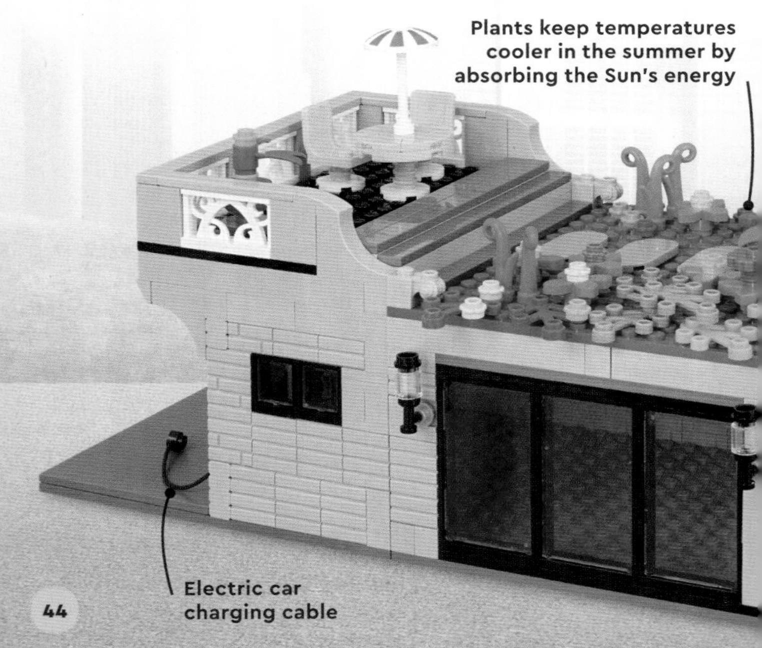

Plants keep temperatures cooler in the summer by absorbing the Sun's energy

Electric car charging cable

IMAGINE!

What do you think a futuristic city would look like? What will the buildings be shaped like? Where will your green spaces go?

BUILD IT!

Add some green-living features to your LEGO houses. You could include a roof garden, car charging port, and solar panels. For solar panels, build plates with bars into your roof and connect the panels using plates with clips.

1×2 tiles on a 4×6 plate

1×2 plate with clip

1×1 plate with bar

Solar energy is converted into electricity, which is stored in a battery

Rooftop plants help lock heat inside in the winter, too

How can we learn about things that are far away?

Scientists have to come up with lots of clever ways to learn about the universe. They can use tools like telescopes to help them see distant objects. They can send spacecraft to take photos and measurements of faraway planets, and they can do experiments in the laboratory to compare how things work on Earth with how they work in space.

Space souvenirs

A sample return is when astronauts or robotic missions bring pieces of things from space, like asteroids or the Moon, back to Earth. Sample returns help scientists figure out how and when these objects formed.

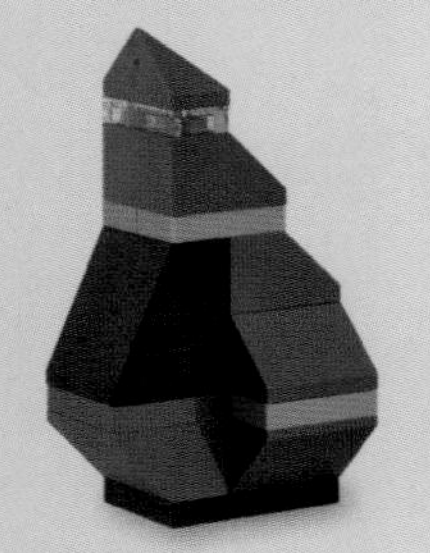

REALLY!
NASA's Apollo missions brought back **382 kg** (842 pounds) of rock from the Moon!

Did you know?

LEGO® Ideas Women of NASA (set 21312) celebrates four scientists who have added to our knowledge of the universe: astronomer Nancy Grace Roman, computer scientist Margaret Hamilton, and astronauts Sally Ride and Mae Jemison.

How can robots help us learn about space?

We use robots to go to places in our Solar System where it is currently too dangerous to send a human, or it would take too long. Some robotic spacecraft or probes fly by an object and send back photos, while others might orbit or even land on it. Scientists can control the craft from Earth, but they have to be patient. Sometimes it can take many years to get there!

IMAGINE!

What would your **LEGO space robot** look like? What would it collect or find?

A new dawn

The Dawn spacecraft was an orbiter mission launched in 2007. It was the first mission ever to orbit two different bodies. It first went to the asteroid Vesta and then to the dwarf planet Ceres.

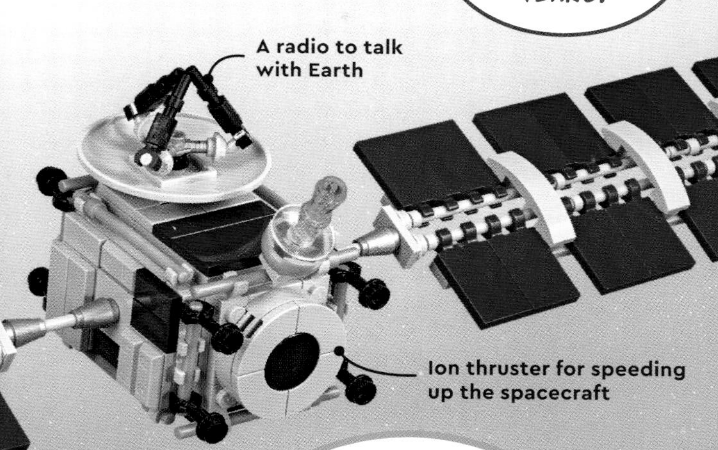

BUILD IT!

You can make a model of the Dawn spacecraft with just a few small pieces! Start with a brick with four side knobs, then add bars and tiles with clips to make the solar arrays.

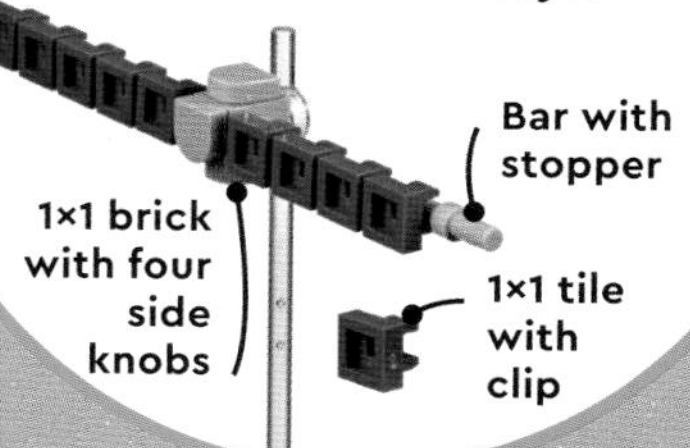

How are rockets launched?

We use rockets to overcome Earth's very strong gravity. To get all the way into orbit, a rocket has to be lifted up faster than gravity can pull it back down. Rockets do this by burning fuel and letting the exhaust from the explosion escape from the back of the rocket. This creates a push called thrust.

WOW! The Space Shuttle was the first-ever **reusable** spacecraft.

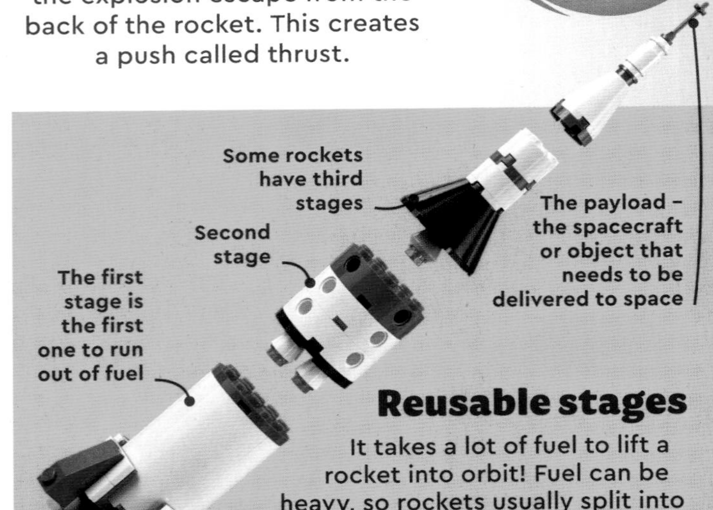

Some rockets have third stages

The payload – the spacecraft or object that needs to be delivered to space

Second stage

The first stage is the first one to run out of fuel

Reusable stages

It takes a lot of fuel to lift a rocket into orbit! Fuel can be heavy, so rockets usually split into parts called stages. Each stage carries fuel. When the fuel gets used up, the stage drops away, to stop it from weighing down the rest of the rocket. Some new rockets are being designed with reusable first stages so that an entirely new rocket doesn't need to be built every time one is launched.

Liquid fuel tank
Solid fuel rocket booster
NASA's now retired Space Shuttle was designed to be used again and again
THIS ROCK-ETS MY WORLD!
Engines produce thrust

Just how **big** do planets get?

Jupiter, Saturn, Uranus, and Neptune are the four giant planets in our Solar System and are known as the Jovian planets. They are mostly made of gas, so unlike terrestrial or dwarf planets they have no solid surfaces to stand on. The biggest giant planet is Jupiter, which is 11 times wider than Earth. It has as much mass (is made up of as much stuff) as 318 Earths. As massive as Jupiter is, scientists think planets outside of our Solar System may be up to 13 times more massive!

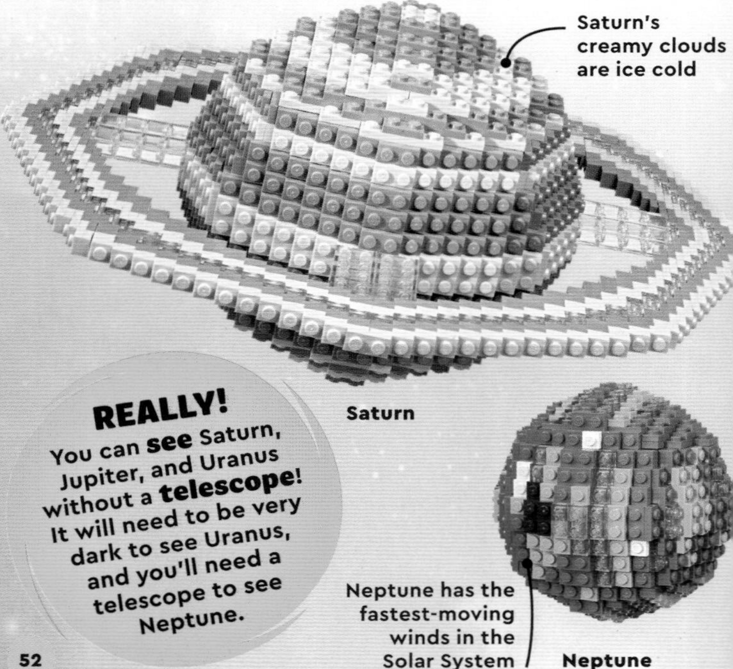

REALLY!

You can **see** Saturn, Jupiter, and Uranus without a **telescope**! It will need to be very dark to see Uranus, and you'll need a telescope to see Neptune.

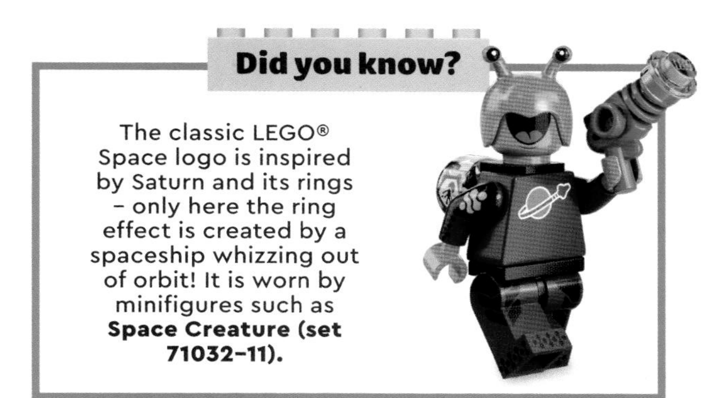

The classic LEGO® Space logo is inspired by Saturn and its rings – only here the ring effect is created by a spaceship whizzing out of orbit! It is worn by minifigures such as **Space Creature (set 71032-11).**

Jupiter

Uranus

Why do stars twinkle?

In space, stars don't twinkle. But when you look at stars from Earth, they appear to do so. This is because we are looking at them through Earth's atmosphere where the air is very thick and moves around. As the light travels through the air it gets distorted, making it seem as if the stars are twinkling. Telescopes in space are above the air, so they can get clearer images.

A star's orbit

Most stars orbit around the centre of their galaxies, just like planets orbit around stars. Because galaxies are so large, it can take stars millions of years to go around just once.

Open places without bright lights are good for stargazing

BUILD IT!

For this scene, star parts are built onto headlight bricks. Leaving the stars off and shining a light from behind creates a different starry effect through the holes in the headlight bricks.

WOW!

One way to tell a planet from a star in the sky is that planets don't **twinkle** as much as stars appear to do.

A cloudless night is best for spotting stars

Telescopes can help you see even more stars

BUILD IT!

This spaceship's wings are more like an insect's than an aeroplane's! A single ball-and-socket joint connects each one at the front, allowing it to twist and turn to suit different conditions.

1×2 plate with ball

Sideways 1×2 plate with socket

Asteroids in the belt are actually very far apart

DIDN'T EXPECT THIS JOURNEY TO BE SO ROCKY!

Some asteroids look like space potatoes!

What is the asteroid belt?

Asteroids are chunks of rock and metal that orbit the Sun, and they are usually uneven in shape. There are millions of asteroids in our Solar System, and most of the known ones are located in the asteroid belt – a vast ring of debris that orbits between Mars and Jupiter. "Asteroid" means "starlike" because although early astronomers knew asteroids were not stars, they looked like stars through small telescopes.

Building blocks

Many asteroids are made from minerals that could be used for building spaceships or space stations in the future. Some asteroids even have water ice that could be used for drinking or making rocket fuel.

IMAGINE!

What would your **spaceship** look like? It would need to be speedy and agile to get through the asteroid belt!

What happens if something falls into a black hole?

Black holes are places in space where the gravity is so strong that nothing can travel fast enough to escape. Before an object falls into a black hole, it is squeezed and squashed by the immense gravity. Sometimes the material falling into a black hole can swirl around it, giving off huge amounts of light before plunging beyond the point of no return, known as the event horizon.

Accretion disc is made of material swirling into the black hole

REALLY!
There is a **supermassive black hole** in the centre of our galaxy called Sagittarius A*.

About time

The closer you get to a black hole, the slower time goes for you from the perspective of Earth. Time will feel normal to you, but for anyone watching you, it would look like you are in slow motion!

Anything that passes beyond the event horizon can't come back out!

Could there be life beyond Earth?

Space is really, REALLY big! There are so many areas to explore. Scientists haven't found any life beyond Earth yet, but there are some great places in our Solar System to look for it. Life might look very different on other planets. However we know that on Earth all life needs liquid water, so finding water in space might help us find life.

IMAGINE!
What might an **alien's vehicle** look like on a frozen planet? Build a cool ride!

Below the surface

The oceans underneath thick layers of ice on worlds like Europa or Pluto would be perfect places to look for life. Who knows what kind of amazing creatures could be swimming around down there?

Could we send a **message** to aliens?

Scientists don't know yet if there is life beyond Earth, let alone if there are other intelligent civilizations out there. If there are, maybe we could find them and send a message saying hello. SETI is the Search for Extraterrestrial Intelligence. SETI scientists have come up with many clever way to look for aliens.

Is anyone there?

Radio waves are a form of light, or electromagnetic radiation, that humans can't see. We can use radio telescopes to observe things in space, like stars and galaxies. Some scientists hope that if alien civilizations use radio waves, maybe we will be able to find them with radio telescopes, like the Arecibo telescope, which was active until 2020.

Numbers 1 through 10

Arecibo message

The Arecibo message was one of several radio messages that scientists sent into space with the hope that someday intelligent aliens might receive one and respond to it! It includes information about humans and Earth's place in the Solar System.

Information about DNA

IMAGINE!
What might **aliens** want to tell us on Earth? Create a message with images.

A stick figure of a human

HELLO! IS ANYBODY THERE?

Map of the Solar System

Drawing of the Arecibo telescope

Can you go on a space holiday?

One day soon, space tourism may be more widely available! Imagine taking a cruise around the Moon, playing in microgravity, or peering back at beautiful blue Earth from high above the atmosphere! What do you think it would be like to play basketball or volleyball in the Moon's low gravity?

Space tourists will use radio to communicate with Earth

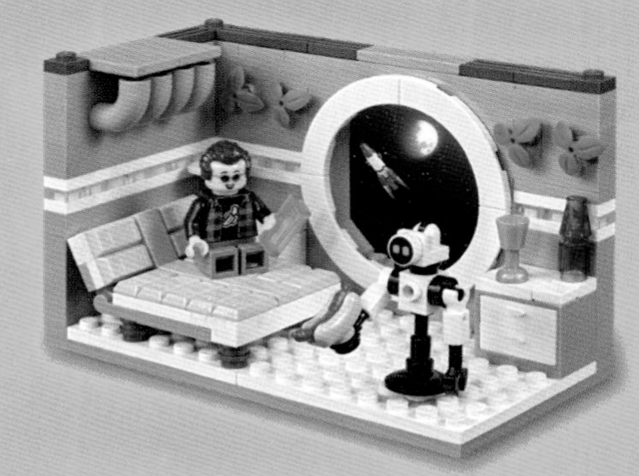

Room with a view

A space hotel would be a space station where guests could stay as they orbited Earth. Most satellites would travel in low Earth orbit (LEO), the region of space closest to Earth. It only takes a satellite in LEO about 90 minutes to go around the planet once, so guests would get to see 16 sunrises and sunsets a day.

Tourists will need air tanks to breathe

I WILL... WHEN IT GETS HERE.

Could humans live on huge space stations?

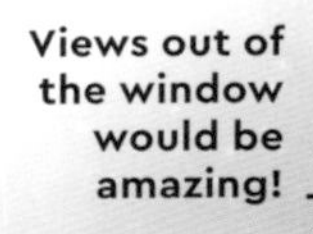

Views out of the window would be amazing!

BUILD IT!

The portals dividing each section of this space station are made from sideways half-arch pieces. The ones at the top are back to back and only connected by clips attached to a bar.

Sideways 1×1 plate with clip

Sideways 1×5×4 half-arch

Bar

In the future, humans could build giant cities orbiting around planets or maybe even around objects like black holes! These cities would need to produce their own power and grow food. They would require places for spaceships to dock and a way to communicate with other stations. Some planets could have lots of stations orbiting around them or maybe just one big station.

IMAGINE!

What would your **dream bedroom** look like in space? What cool things would it have? Build a cosy pod!

Could we make other planets more like Earth?

Changing a planet to be more like Earth is called terraforming. Many scientists are excited about the idea of terraforming Mars. Mars is very similar to Earth, so it might be easier to terraform than other planets. To terraform Mars, humans would need to thicken the atmosphere so that Mars could stay warmer. Once Mars warmed up, the water ice at its poles could melt and create oceans, rivers, and lakes.

Asteroids

Other places to terraform might be the inside of asteroids! They could be hollowed out and made to spin. The spin could create artificial gravity, and the hollow asteroid could be filled with air, soil, water, and living things.

REALLY!
Giant mirrors in space could direct light to Mars and make it warmer.

Could there be a multiverse?

Scientists have many ideas about the nature of our universe. To find out which ones are true, they need to find evidence or clues. One idea scientists want to find evidence for is the multiverse, which is the concept that there could be more universes than ours. So far we don't know, but we are still investigating. Parallel universe theory explores the possibility that there might be nearby universes that are almost complete copies of our own.

IMAGINE!

What might a **parallel universe** look like? Build an everyday scene on Earth... but with a few strange differences!

BUILD IT!

Make a pair of parallel worlds by building two almost mirror-image scenes with distinct differences. Here, one reality is black and white and inhabited by minifigure wolves!

Meet the authors

Jennifer Swanson

Jennifer is an award-winning author of multiple STEM (science, technology, engineering, and maths) books for children.

Why did you choose to write about Earth and STEM subjects?
I love to encourage readers to notice the science in the world around them – it's everywhere! And with this book, you can also *build* it.

What advice do you have for children who want to write?
Write about something that you love, that you're curious about, and that you are excited to share with others. But most of all, have fun!

If you could visit anywhere on Earth or in space, where would you go?
I would go to the Marianas Trench in the Pacific Ocean. I am fascinated by the amazing and unique creatures that are found in the deep, dark ocean.

Arwen Hubbard

Arwen is an ecologist, space science educator, writer, and podcaster.

Why did you choose to write about space?
Because it is so fascinating! I love sharing the amazing things scientists have learned. We have discovered things we never even imagined and there is so much more to explore.

What advice do you have for children who want to write?
The key to writing is practice! The more you write, the better you get. It helps to find a topic you are passionate about.

If you could visit anywhere on Earth or in space, where would you go?
If I could go anywhere in the universe, I would want to visit Pluto and see its amazing features made from ice, like towering mountains and gigantic shield volcanoes.

Meet the model designers

The inspirational models in this book were created by a talented group of model designers who love to build with LEGO® bricks. We asked four of the model designers some questions about their creative process.

Tim Goddard

What is your top building tip?

If you are recreating a real object, look at lots of references, but don't worry too much about fitting in every detail. Focus on the main things that are characteristic of what you are building.

If you were a minifigure, which of the builds in this book would you like to visit or try out?

Playing volleyball on the Moon (pages 64–5) would be great fun! With low gravity, you can jump really high!

Jason Briscoe

What is your top building tip?

Build as much as you can and every day if possible. The more you build and learn about how bricks connect in different ways, the better you become.

Simon Pickard

How do your plan your LEGO models?
I source reference images and select the key component or most challenging feature as a starting point. Then it's a creative process of trial and error to get it just right.

What is your top building tip?
Never compromise – there is always a solution to achieve the perfect look.

If you could build anything in space, what would you build?
I'd love to build more historical scenes of space exploration.

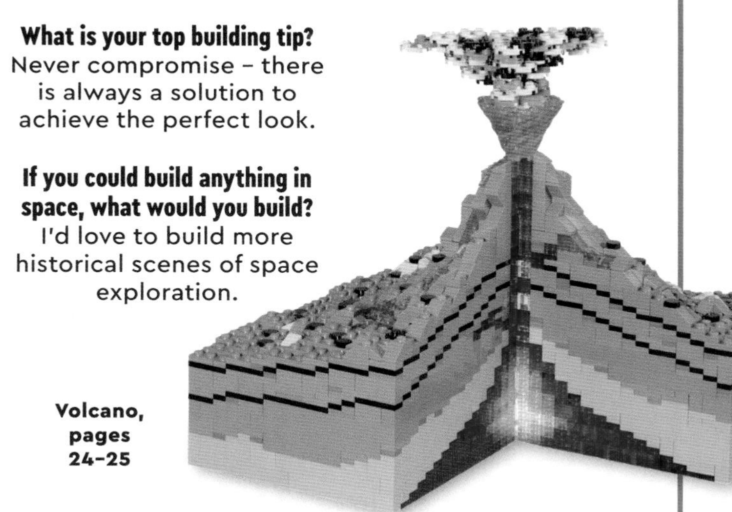

Volcano, pages 24–25

Nate Dias

How do your plan your LEGO models?
I usually plan them on a computer. I get an idea in my head and go with it. The computer makes it easier for me to change the models if I need to, without taking the whole model apart.

Glossary

artificial gravity
The creation of a force in a spacecraft that mimics gravity. This could be achieved by spinning a spacecraft.

asteroid
A chunk of rock smaller than a planet, which orbits the Sun.

atmosphere
The layer of gases that surround a planet.

atom
A tiny piece of an element. Everything in the universe is made from atoms.

black hole
An area in space with incredibly strong gravity that means even light is pulled into it. Consequently, we can't see a black hole.

crust
The thin, outermost layer of Earth, made up or rocks and minerals.

dwarf planet
An object that is much smaller than a planet like Earth but is big enough to have a round shape. Like a planet, it orbits the Sun.

ecosystem
Plants and animals that rely on each other and the environment they share.

element
A substance that cannot be broken down into anything simpler without losing its characteristics.

equator
The imaginary line that runs around the widest part of a planet.

galaxy
A group of billions of stars that, along with gas and dust, all move together in space. There are billions of galaxies.

gas
A material made up of atoms or small groups of atoms that are loosely scattered through space.

gravity
The force that pulls things together. Gravity makes Earth orbit the Sun and the Moon orbit Earth.

habitat
The environment where an animal lives.

inner Solar System
The part of the Solar System that includes everything up to and including the asteroid belt. Earth, Mercury, Venus, and Mars are in this.

low Earth orbit (LEO)
An orbit area that is very close to Earth.

mass
A measure of the amount of matter in an object.

matter
The stuff that things are made from.

meteor
A lump or rock or dust that burns up as it enters Earth's atmosphere.

mineral
A naturally occurring nonliving solid made up of specific combinations of chemical elements.

microgravity
The reduced strength of gravity that objects experience in orbit, making them appear weightless.

moon
Any natural object that orbits around a planet.

NASA
The National Aeronautics and Space Administration (NASA) is a part of the US government that explores air and space. It was established in October 1958.

nebula
A giant cloud of dust and gas in space.

orbit
The path that one object makes around a more massive object in space. It happens because of gravity.

plateau
A flat piece of land that is higher than the land next to it.

predator
An animal that hunts other animals for food.

radiation
Energy that moves in waves.

satellite
Any object that orbits around a planet. Moons are natural satellites, but people have put many artificial ones into orbit around Earth.

Solar System
The Sun and everything that orbits around it.

universe
Everything that exists, including all the planets, stars, and galaxies.

Senior Editor Helen Murray
Project Art Editor Jenny Edwards
Senior Production Editor Jennifer Murray
Senior Production Controller Mandy Inness
Managing Editor Paula Regan
Managing Art Editor Jo Connor
Managing Director Mark Searle

Inspirational models built by Simon Pickard, Tim Goddard, Nate Dias, and Jason Briscoe
Additional models built by Jessica Farrell, Rod Gillies, Barney Main, James McKeag, Emily Corl, and Kevin Hall

Photography by Gary Ombler
Additional LEGO text by Laura Gilbert, Simon Hugo, and Helen Murray
Geography consultant David Holmes
Space consultant Giles Sparrow

DK would like to thank:
Randi Sørensen, Ashley Blais, Heidi K. Jensen, Martin Leighton Lindhart, and Nina Koopmann at the LEGO Group. DK also thanks Laura Gilbert for editorial support, Isabelle Merry for design support, and Julia March for proofreading.

First published in Great Britain in 2025 by Dorling Kindersley Limited, 20 Vauxhall Bridge Road, London SW1V 2SA

Contains content previously published in LEGO® *Amazing Earth* (2023) and LEGO® *Amazing Space* (2024).

The authorised representative in the EEA is Dorling Kindersley Verlag GmbH. Arnulfstr. 124, 80636 Munich, Germany

Manufactured by Dorling Kindersley, 20 Vauxhall Bridge Road, London SW1V 2SA, UK under licence from the LEGO Group.

10 9 8 7 6 5 4 3 2 1
001-349503-Feb/2025

A CIP catalogue record for this book is available from the British Library.
978-0-2417-4085-9

Printed and bound in China

www.dk.com
www.LEGO.com

MIX
Paper | Supporting responsible forestry
FSC™ C018179

This book was made with Forest Stewardship Council™ certified paper – one small step in DK's commitment to a sustainable future.
Learn more at www.dk.com/uk/information/sustainability